Paper Republic LLC
7548 Ravenna Ave NE, Seattle, Washington 98115
Text and illustration copyright © 2014 by Chao Wang
Simplified Chinese-English edition copyright © 2016 by China Educational Publications Import & Export Corporation Ltd.
Publication Consultant: Roxanne Hsu Feldman
Published by Paper Republic LLC, by arrangement with Phoenix Juvenile and Children's Publishing Ltd.
All rights reserved, including the right of reproduction in whole or in part in any form.
Printed and bound in China.
ISBN 978-1-945-29510-2

The art for this book was created digitally.
For more titles from Candied Plums and additional features, please visit www.candiedplums.com.

变变变
ALAKAZAM

by **Chao Wang**
translated by **Duncan Poupard**

Candied Plums

你好，大手掌！

nǐ hǎo　dà shǒu zhǎng

nǐ hǎo xiǎo shǒu zhǎng
你好，小手掌！
wǒ men yì qǐ lái wán yóu xì ba
我们一起来玩游戏吧。

zhāng kāi shǒu zhǐ　　tú shàng yán sè

张开手指，涂上颜色，

biàn　　biàn　　biàn

变，变，变！

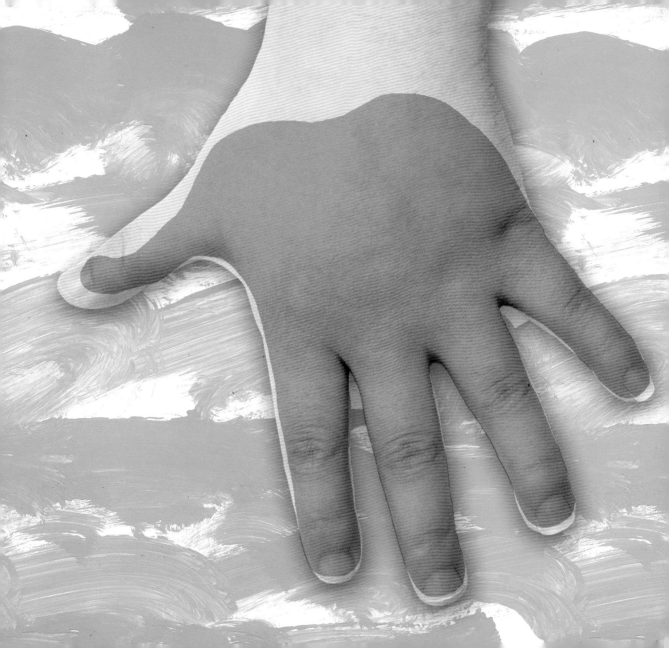

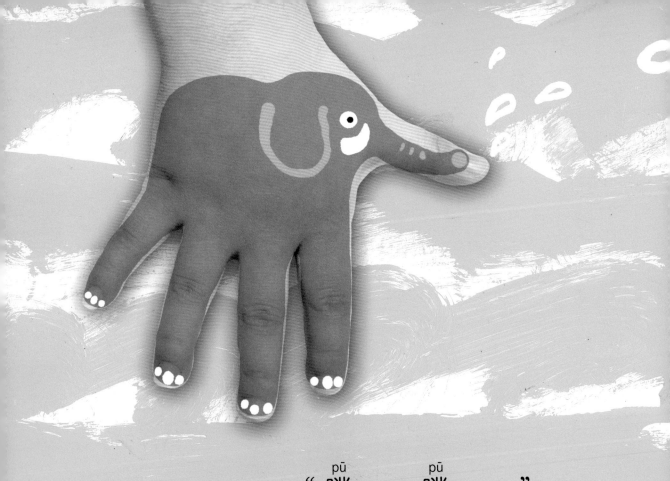

"噗——噗——"

xiàng bǎo bao hé xiàng bà ba pēn shuǐ la
象宝宝和象爸爸喷水啦!

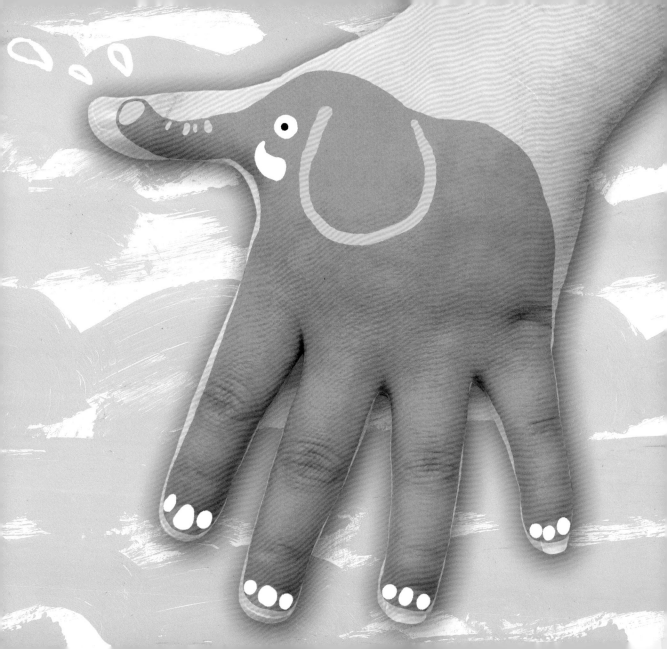

huàn yì zhǒng yán sè ba

换一种颜色吧——

bìan bìan bìan

变，变，变！

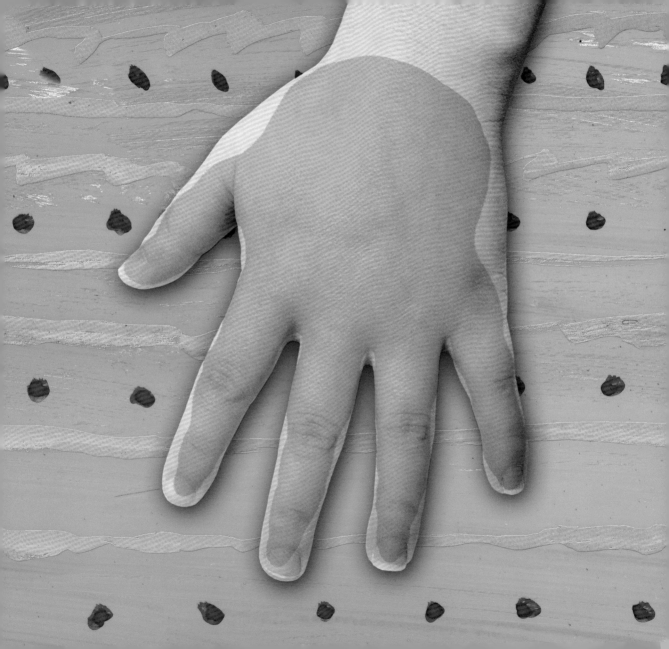

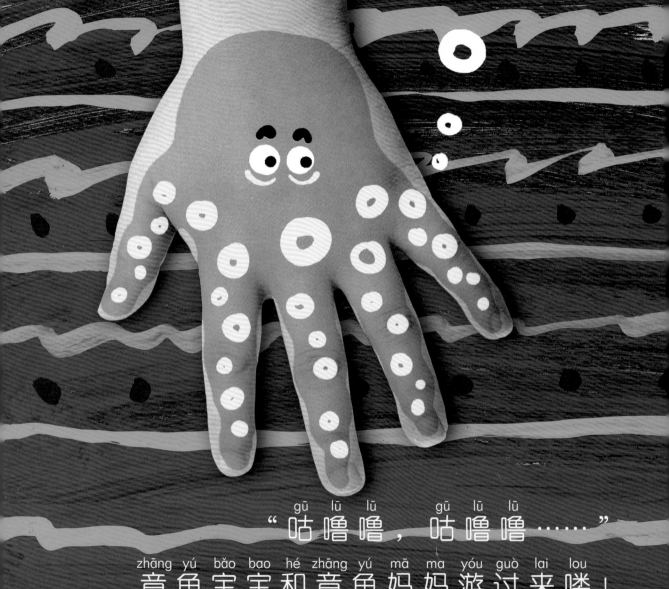

"咕噜噜，咕噜噜……"
章鱼宝宝和章鱼妈妈游过来喽！

huàn gè shǒu shì shì shi kàn
换个手势试试看——
biàn　　biàn　　biàn
变，变，变！

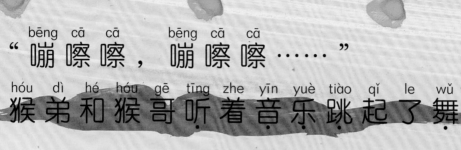

"<ruby>嘣<rt>bēng</rt></ruby><ruby>嚓<rt>cā</rt></ruby><ruby>嚓<rt>cā</rt></ruby>，<ruby>嘣<rt>bēng</rt></ruby><ruby>嚓<rt>cā</rt></ruby><ruby>嚓<rt>cā</rt></ruby>……"

<ruby>猴<rt>hóu</rt></ruby><ruby>弟<rt>dì</rt></ruby><ruby>和<rt>hé</rt></ruby><ruby>猴<rt>hóu</rt></ruby><ruby>哥<rt>gē</rt></ruby><ruby>听<rt>tīng</rt></ruby><ruby>着<rt>zhe</rt></ruby><ruby>音<rt>yīn</rt></ruby><ruby>乐<rt>yuè</rt></ruby><ruby>跳<rt>tiào</rt></ruby><ruby>起<rt>qǐ</rt></ruby><ruby>了<rt>le</rt></ruby><ruby>舞<rt>wǔ</rt></ruby>！

再换个手势呢——
变，变，变！

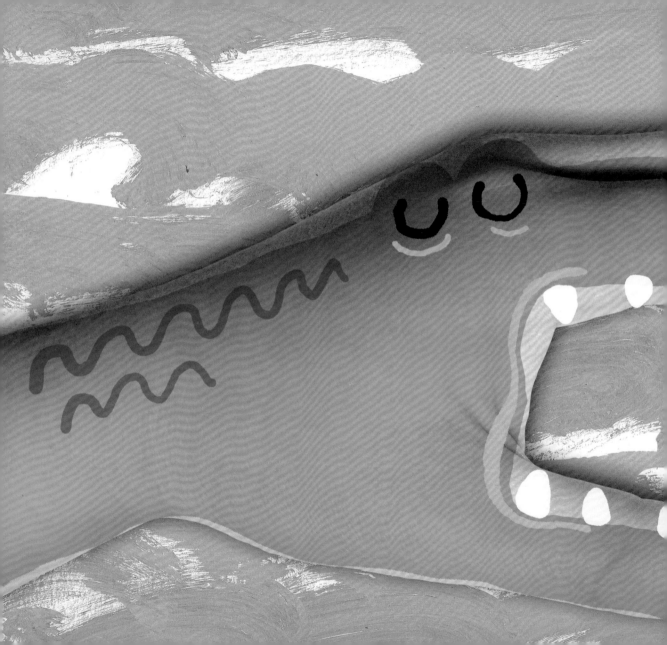